Santa Claus
Is Coming To Town

Classic Holiday Collection

written by Dandi
illustrated by Tammie Speer-Lyon

Max kicked at a snow bank as he watched his big sister, Jennifer, play with her friends. Why couldn't she play with him? Finally he shouted, "Jennifer! I want to make a snowman NOW!

"Don't shout, Max," Jennifer called to him. And she went back to her snowball fight.

Max didn't understand. Why shouldn't he shout outside where the snow could swallow his shout?

Max plopped down on the step to pout. Just then, a stray snowball landed smack on Max's nose!

"Mom!" he cried, running into the house. "A snowball hit me!" Max told his mother. And although it didn't really hurt, Max started to cry. Max's mother kissed him.

"Better not cry," she said gently.

"Shall I tell you why?"

Now Max *was* confused! He tried to think.

You better not shout. . .

You better not pout. . .

Better not cry. . .

I'm telling you why. . .

Max remembered.

"Santa Claus!" he shouted.

Then in a whisper, "Santa Claus is coming to town."

Max knew he probably hadn't made Santa's list of good boys and girls this year. Take the time his cousin slept over. Max kicked him out of bed. Not exactly *nice*.

When Max had watered Mother's flowers with juice, it had seemed funny. . . until the flowers died. That wasn't so nice either.

"Jennifer," Max asked when she came in, "Do you think I've been naughty or nice this year?"

"Well," Jennifer said, grinning. "You did stick gum in my hair while I was sleeping. It sure didn't *feel* nice when Mom had to cut it out."

Max had to face it. Santa Claus might be coming to town, but he probably wouldn't stop at Max's stocking. Christmas Eve, Max and Jennifer put tinsel on the tree. "Tonight's the night Santa Claus is coming to town," Jennifer said. "Aren't you excited, Max!" But Max knew he had been more naughty than nice this year. Santa wouldn't leave anything for him.

Max imagined Santa and his reindeer flying from house to house. It would be hard work carrying that pouch down so many chimneys. Santa must get awfully tired. "Mom," Max called, "Could I have some milk and cookies, please?"

"It's awfully late," Mother answered.

"They're not for me," said Max. Max set out a big glass of cold milk and four Christmas cookies he had decorated himself.

Max woke up first on Christmas morning. He crept downstairs in darkness, afraid to look at his stocking. He knew it would be empty.

Light from the treetop angel fell on the mantel. There, to his surprise, Max saw his own Christmas stocking bulging with gifts from Santa. Sticking out at the top was a note:

Dear Max,

Thanks for the treat!

What you did was very nice!

Merry Christmas!

Love,

Santa

"I was NICE!" Max shouted. And he ran through the house, waking up his family, singing:

"He made up his list, and checked it all twice.
Santa decided Max could be nice!
Santa Claus is coming to town."